LEAD SHEETS
Real Key & Capo

MY SOUL AMONG LIONS

PSALMS 11–20

WARHORN
MEDIA

Published 2017 by Warhorn Media

All songs from the album *Psalms 11–20*
by My Soul Among Lions (MySoulAmongLions.com)
available from Warhorn Media

Cover design by Ben Crum
Engraving and interior layout by Alex McNeilly

Warhorn Media
2401 S Endwright Rd.
Bloomington, IN 47403
WarhornMedia.com

Lead sheets available for free download at ClearnoteSongbook.com
Recordings available for free streaming at ClearnoteSongbook.com

Printed in the United States of America
21   20   19   18   17   1   2   3   4   5

ISBN-13: 978-1-940017-15-0
ISBN-10: 1-940017-15-7

CONTENTS

MY SOUL AMONG LIONS

PSALMS 11–20

Come Now, My Friend
— PSALM 11 —

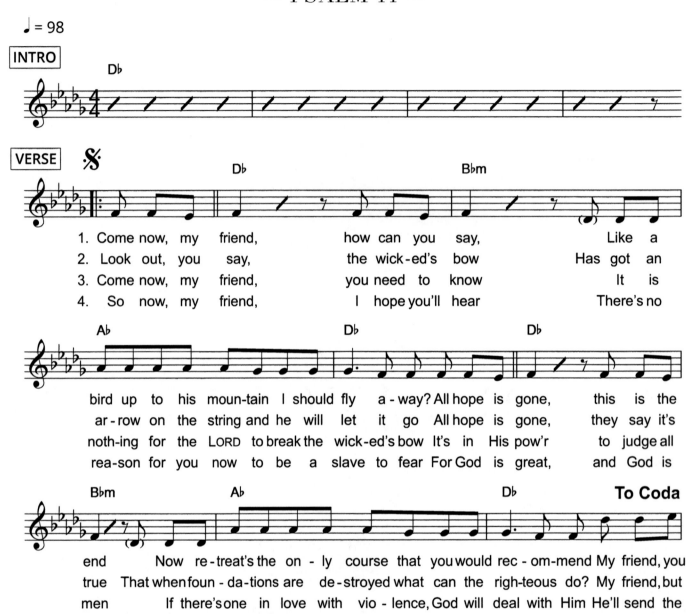

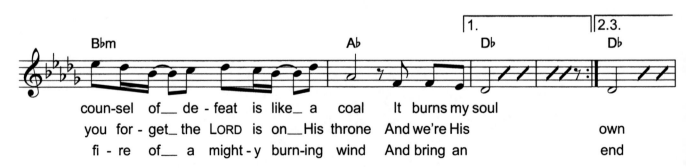

Lyrics and music by JODY KILLINGSWORTH

Come Now, My Friend
— PSALM 11 —

CAPO I

Lyrics and music by JODY KILLINGSWORTH

Refuge
— PSALM 11 —

REAL KEY

♩ = 92

INTRO | D#m B A#m | D#m B A#m |

VERSE

D#m — B — A#m

1. In the LORD I take ref - uge
2. "I've seen the wick - ed's bow bend - ing
3. In the LORD I take ref - uge
4. To God who judg - es the righ - teous

D#m — B — A#m

How can you say to my soul:
I hear he's search - ing for you
Why do you coun - sel de - spair
Whose righ - teous soul burns with hate

B — F# — D#m — C#

"Fly like a bird far a - way to your moun - tain
With all a - round the foun - da - tions up - end - ing
When all a - round us the signs of God's bless - ings
When He dis - cov - ers the lov - ers of vio - lence

B — F# — C# — D#m — B

Ain't noth - ing left here but woe   Head for the hills and let's go
And us with num - bers so few   What can the righ - teous
Form mon - u - ments to His care?   Lift up your hearts in
And pours His wrath on their pate   O they de - serve their

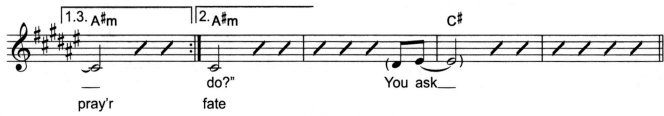

1.3. A#m | 2. A#m | | C#

__   pray'r
do?"   fate
You ask__

6 Lyrics by JODY KILLINGSWORTH and JAKE MENTZEL. Music by JODY KILLINGSWORTH.

Refuge
— PSALM 11 —

Lyrics by JODY KILLINGSWORTH and JAKE MENTZEL. Music by JODY KILLINGSWORTH.

CAPO VI

CHORUS

F   Csus   C

1. But the LORD is in His ho-ly tem - - ple_____
2. For the LORD is in His ho-ly tem - - ple_____
3. For the LORD is in His ho-ly tem - - ple_____

F   C

God is on His throne high in His heav'n___
God is on His throne high in His heav'n___
God is on His throne high in His heav'n___

F   Csus   C

What His eyes be - hold would make you trem - ble He
What His eyes be - hold would make you trem - ble He
What His eyes be - hold would make you trem - ble He

G

| 1. | D.C. | 2. | 3. |

sees the hearts__ of man__
sees your ev - 'ry plan__
knows the hearts__ of man__

1st x back to INTRO   *2nd x* repeat CHORUS

VERSE   Am   F   Em   Am   F

5. In the LORD I take ref - uge   And plead the blood of His grace

Em   F   C   Am   G

___ No more a rea - son to fear___ the un - righ - teous

F   C   G   Am   F

For they will end_ in dis - grace__   But we will see_ His

Em   G   C

face

The Words of the LORD
— PSALM 12 —

REAL KEY

♩ = 102

CHORUS

The words of the LORD are pure words Like sil-ver tried in a fur-nace The
words of the LORD are pure words Re-fined___ for sev-en times   I don't much care for
your words You speak and I___ get ner-vous   The   words of the LORD are
pure words I keep them in___ my mind___

VERSE

1.   Help, LORD, for the god-ly man   ceas-es   to   be   The
2. The wick-ed strut on ev-'ry side,   taunt-ing with_ their boasts   "There
3. He sees the poor are plun-dered and He hears the need-y groan   God

faith-ful have all   left the land,_ there's none that I___   can   see
is no help for   him in God,_   not   from the LORD of Hosts"   But
will a-rise a-gain in pow'r_   and   take them for_   His   own   But

Ev-'ry-where I   go now   all   I hear is van-i-ty_____   The
I will trust my   Fa-ther God, the Son, and Ho-ly Ghost___
ly-ing lips_ and crook-ed hearts, our LORD has nev-er known___   He

Lyrics by JODY KILLINGSWORTH and JAKE MENTZEL. Music by JODY KILLINGSWORTH.

The Words of the LORD
— PSALM 12 —

CHORUS

The words of the LORD are pure words Like sil-ver tried in a fur-nace The
words of the LORD are pure words Re-fined___ for sev-en times I don't much care for
your words You speak and I___ get ner-vous The words of the LORD are
pure words I keep them in___ my mind___

VERSE

1. Help, LORD, for the god-ly man ceas-es to be The
2. The wick-ed strut on ev-'ry side, taunt-ing with their boasts "There
3. He sees the poor are plun-dered and He hears the need-y groan God

faith-ful have all left the land, there's none that I___ can see
is no help for him in God, not from the LORD of Hosts" But
will a-rise a-gain in pow'r and take them for___ His own But

Ev-'ry-where I go now all I hear is van-i-ty_____ The
I will trust my Fa-ther God, the Son, and Ho-ly Ghost___
ly-ing lips_ and crook-ed hearts, our LORD has nev-er known___ He

Lyrics by JODY KILLINGSWORTH and JAKE MENTZEL. Music by JODY KILLINGSWORTH.

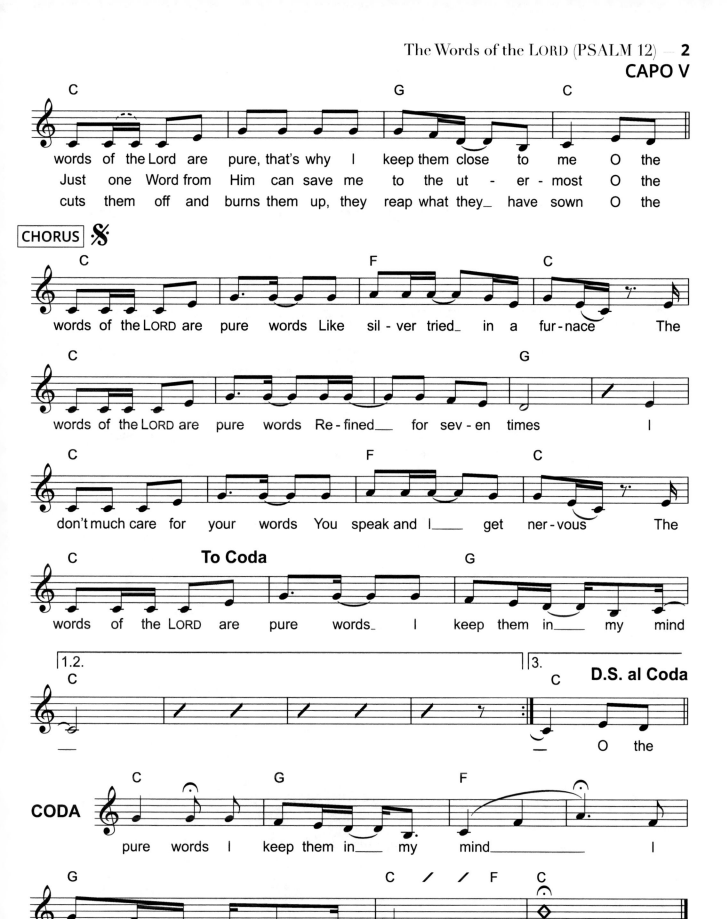

How Long, O Lord?
— PSALM 13 —

Lyrics by JODY KILLINGSWORTH and JAKE MENTZEL. Music by JODY KILLINGSWORTH.

INTERLUDE

Cm — Fm — Bb — Cm — Fm — Bb

Cm — Gm/Bb — Gm — Ab — Bb — Cm

VERSE

Cm — Fm — Bb — Cm

3. How long, O____ LORD? I am fight-ing__ for sur-viv - al If my

Fm — Bb — Cm — Gm/Bb — Gm

eyes don't see re-viv - al Then I__ will sleep the bit-ter sleep of

Ab — Bb — Eb — **D.S. al Coda**

death How__ long, O____ LORD?____

CHORUS — Ab — Eb — Bb

CODA

How long, O LORD?_____ For all__ my hope's in You Send Your

Ab — Eb — Bb — Ab — Ab — Bb

love,____ don't let__ it be un-true I will sing;____ it's what You said to

Cm — Ab — Bb — Eb

do Re-turn to me;__ How__ long, O____ LORD?__

Ab — Bb — Eb

When will it be?__ How__ long, O____ LORD?__

How Long, O Lord?
— PSALM 13 —

♩ = 80

INTRO

VERSE

1. How long, O____ LORD? Will You hide Your_ face for-ev - er? Will we
2. How long, O____ LORD? Will my heart be_drowned in sor - row? If I

talk no_ more to-geth - er? I strain my ear but hear my thoughts a -
lose more ground to-mor - row My foes_ will think that they have o - ver

1. lone How_ long, O____ LORD?
2. come How_ long, O____ LORD?

CHORUS

How long, O LORD?_____ For I___ have trust - ed You Send Your
love,____ don't let it be un - true I will sing_____ for mer - cies I once
knew Re - turn to me; how_ long, O____ LORD?_

To Coda

Lyrics by JODY KILLINGSWORTH and JAKE MENTZEL. Music by JODY KILLINGSWORTH.

O Savior, Come
— PSALM 14 —

Lyrics by JAKE MENTZEL and PHILIP MOYER. Music by PHILIP MOYER.

O Savior, Come
— PSALM 14 —

Lyrics by JAKE MENTZEL and PHILIP MOYER. Music by PHILIP MOYER.

CHORUS

1st x back to INTERLUDE

2nd x repeat CHORUS

Your Holy Hill
— PSALM 15 —

Lyrics by JODY KILLINGSWORTH and JAKE MENTZEL. Music by JODY KILLINGSWORTH.

Your Holy Hill
— PSALM 15 —

Lyrics by JODY KILLINGSWORTH and JAKE MENTZEL. Music by JODY KILLINGSWORTH.

Your Holy Hill
— PSALM 15 —

♩ = 71

INTRO

D · · G D · · D · · G D A

CHORUS

D · · · G · · D · ·

O___ LORD,_____ who may a - bide__ in Your tent? Who may

G · · A · · D · · A · · D · ·

dwell_ on Your ho - ly____ hill?____ O___ LORD,_____ Who may a -

1.2.3.

G · · D · · G · · A · · D · · G D

bide in Your tent? Who may dwell on Your ho - ly____ hill?

VERSE

G · · D · · A · · D · · G · · D · · A

1. He who walks with in - teg - ri - ty All his works are righ - teous - ness__ Who
2. He who loves all his neigh - bors well Does no wrong un - to his____ friends_ Who
3. He who swears un - to his own hurt And who nev - er takes a____ bribe He's

G · · D · · A · · Bm · · G · · A · · D · · A

speaks the truth deep with - in his heart Does not slan - der with his____ lips____
hon - ors all those who fear the LORD But the wick - ed he con - demns_
hon - est in ev - 'ry - thing he does Nev - er moves or turns a - side____

4.

D · · · A · ·

hill?

5.

D · · · ·

hill?

Lyrics by JODY KILLINGSWORTH and JAKE MENTZEL. Music by JODY KILLINGSWORTH.

Fullness of Joy
— PSALM 16 —

REAL KEY

Lyrics and music by JODY KILLINGSWORTH

Fullness of Joy
— PSALM 16 —

♩ = 73

INTRO

G   Am⁷   Bm   C   G²   Am⁹   Bm⁷   C

G   C   G   C   G   D

VERSE

G   C   D   G

1. O God, my ref - uge   And my pro - tec - tion
2. When men to i - dols pray   They choose cor - rup - tion
3. You are my por - tion   My cup of bles - sing
4. With You be - side me, God   I'm nev - er sha - ken

G   C   D   G   C

I have no oth - er good be - sides___   Your saints who dwell on earth
And cast their Mak - er God a - side___   I won't join in their way
The lines for me_ all plea - sant fall___   So I will praise Your name
My heart and flesh will dwell se - cure___   And e - ven in the grave

B   Em   C   D | 1.3. G   D | 2.4. G   D |

Get my af - fec - tion   In them is all of my_ de - light___
For it's de - struc - tion   Their sor - rows now be mul - ti - plied
with loud pro - fes - sing   When I Your ben - e - fits_ re - call___
I'm not for - sa - ken   You make Your Ho - ly One en - dure

28

Hear a Just Cause
— PSALM 17 —

REAL KEY

♩ = 88, swing ♪s

INTRO

Gm

VERSE 1

Gm

1. Hear a just cause, O my LORD   Give to Your man his right re-ward, O

Dm   Gm

LORD_____   Hear a just cause, O LORD__

Gm

Turn Your face_   and fix Your eyes   See my_ lips_ that they're free of   lies,_ O

Dm   Gm

LORD_____   Hear a just cause, O LORD__

CHORUS

Cm   Gm

Try my   heart   and find that it's right_   Watch my   life both day and   night_ From

Dm   Gm   G

first   to   last__   my feet hold   fast   to   Your_____   ways

Cm   Gm

Seek me, save me, show me Your love_   Spread Your wings a-round me, LORD, from a-bove, O

VERSE 2

CHORUS

REAL KEY

SOLO

| Cm | Gm | Dm | Gm | G |

| Cm | Gm | Dm | Gm |

VERSE 3

Gm

3. Bow-ing down to their gold-en cows Men are try-ing to have their best life now, O

Dm — Gm

LORD_____ Hear a just cause, O LORD__ But

Gm

as for me,_ I have not slipped You've been hold-ing me fast_ by the word of Your lips, O

Dm — Gm

LORD_____ Hear a just cause, O LORD__

CHORUS

Cm — Gm

Try my heart_ and find that it's right_ Watch my life both day and night_ From

Dm — Gm — G

first to last,__ my feet hold fast to Your_____ ways

Cm — Gm

Seek me, save me, show me Your face_ I'll be hap-py in You_ when I a - wake, O

REAL KEY

Hear a Just Cause
— PSALM 17 —

♩ = 88, swing ♪s

INTRO — Em

VERSE 1 — Em

1. Hear a just cause, O my LORD   Give to Your man his right re - ward, O

Bm ... Em

LORD_____   Hear a just cause, O LORD__

Em

Turn Your face_ and fix Your eyes   See my_ lips_ that they're free of lies,_ O

Bm ... Em

LORD_____   Hear a just cause, O LORD__

CHORUS — Am ... Em

Try my heart and find that it's right_   Watch my life both day and night_ From

Bm ... Em   E

first to last__ my feet hold fast to Your_____ ways

Am ... Em

Seek me, save me, show me Your love Spread_ Your wings around me, LORD, from a - bove, O

Lyrics by NATHAN ALBERSON and JODY KILLINGSWORTH. Music by JODY KILLINGSWORTH.

CAPO III

CAPO III

LORD_____ Hear a just cause, O LORD__ I'm

CHORUS

look-ing to You_ in the time of my need An-swer me, LORD, You who lis-ten to me_ The

wick-ed lurks_ like a li-on deep_ in his hid-ing place

Seek me, save me, show me Your love Spread Your wings a-round me, LORD, from a-bove, O
Seek me, save me, don't let me die_ Keep_ me as the ap-ple, LORD, of Your eye, O

1. Em E 2. Em

LORD_____ Hear a just cause, O LORD__ _ O

LORD,_____ hear a just cause, O LORD__ O

LORD,_____ hear a just cause, O LORD

The LORD Is My Refuge
— PSALM 18 —

♩ = 87, swing ♪s

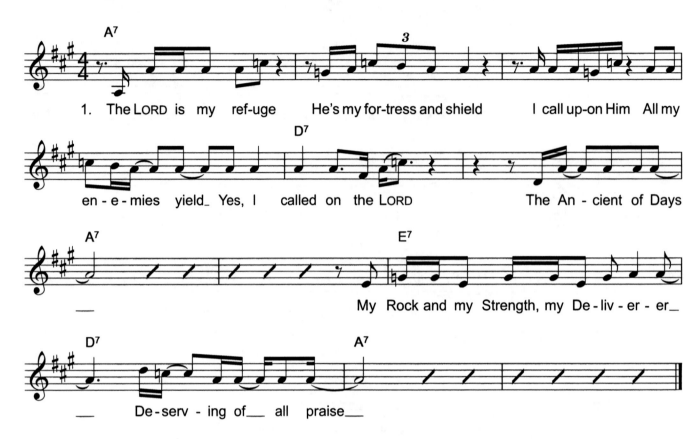

1. The LORD is my ref-uge   He's my for-tress and shield   I call up-on Him   All my en-e-mies yield_ Yes, I called on the LORD   The An - cient of Days __   My Rock and my Strength, my De - liv - er - er_ __ De-serv - ing of__ all   praise__

2. The cords of death around me
   Ruination on my head
   The pains of hell within me
   Left me for dead
   And I called on the LORD
   I cried in my distress
   He heard me from up in His temple
   And He answered my request

3. Then the earth shook and trembled
   And the mountains were rocked
   Fire rained in the heavens
   When His wrath was unlocked
   He mounted the wings of His cherub
   And bowed the heavens down
   Deep darkness was swirling around Him
   Hot flames licked up the ground

4. The heavens roared with thunder
   From a blast of His breath
   Smoke went up from His nostrils
   The skies were painted in death
   The sea gave up her secrets
   Laid her foundations bare
   He chased them all down with His arrows
   Led them right into His snare

5. The LORD reached down from heaven
   Took me up in His arms
   Drew me out of deep waters
   And He saved me from harm
   He's been my strong salvation
   In great calamity
   He brought me out into green pastures
   For He delighted in me

38   Lyrics by JAKE MENTZEL. Music by JODY KILLINGSWORTH and PHILIP MOYER.

6. I've set the LORD before me
Kept all His commands
And He has well rewarded
My pure heart and clean hands
I have kept the ways of God
I have not strayed from His side
The wicked keep moving and shifting
But with Him I will abide

7. To the kind He is kind
To the pure He is pure
To the upright He's blameless
And all His mercies are sure
But to the crooked and proud
They only know His dread
He saves a humble people
But He kills them wicked dead

8. You light up my lamp
You chase away my night
Though a host should come against me
I'll be filled with Your might
My God, His way, it is perfect
And every word of His is true
My LORD, You're a shield and a refuge
For every man who trusts in You

9. Who is God, but the LORD?
Is there a rock like You?
If You train my hands for war
What can my enemies do?
You set my feet securely
I'm like a deer upon the heights
I bend back my bow of solid bronze
And set the wicked in my sights

10. Your salvation's my shield
And my support is Your hand
My feet won't slip or stumble
In such a broad and stable land
Your gentleness and mercy
It's what has made me great
Your way is sure before me
And all my paths are good and straight

11. I'll run down my foes
They will all be consumed
When they see me coming
They'll know that they are doomed
And though they cry out for help
Still they'll fall beneath my feet
To the wind I'll scatter their ashes
And drag their bodies through the streets

12. You've delivered me from strife
Put the nations in my sway
And though they have not known me
I know that they'll obey
They come to me and they tremble
Down on their hands and on their knees
I receive them into my service
I'm accepting of their pleas

13. The LORD is my refuge
And blessed be my Rock
A good and faithful Shepherd
Who saves His little flock
He delivers us from evil
And takes away our enemies
He rescues us from the violent
And puts our restless hearts at ease

14. I'll praise You to the heathen
Declare to them Your fame
You bring Your king salvation
And Jesus is His name
And now I'll praise His name forever
And bring to Him my offerings
Jesus loves and cares for His children
He's our gracious King of kings

The LORD Is My Refuge
— PSALM 18 —

DGDGBD
CAPO II

♩ = 87, swing ♪s

1. The LORD is my ref-uge   He's my for-tress and shield   I call up-on Him   All my en - e - mies yield_ Yes, I called on the LORD   The An - cient of Days   _ My Rock and my Strength, my De - liv - er - er_ _ De - serv - ing of__ all praise__

2. The cords of death around me
Ruination on my head
The pains of hell within me
Left me for dead
And I called on the LORD
I cried in my distress
He heard me from up in His temple
And He answered my request

3. Then the earth shook and trembled
And the mountains were rocked
Fire rained in the heavens
When His wrath was unlocked
He mounted the wings of His cherub
And bowed the heavens down
Deep darkness was swirling around Him
Hot flames licked up the ground

4. The heavens roared with thunder
From a blast of His breath
Smoke went up from His nostrils
The skies were painted in death
The sea gave up her secrets
Laid her foundations bare
He chased them all down with His arrows
Led them right into His snare

5. The LORD reached down from heaven
Took me up in His arms
Drew me out of deep waters
And He saved me from harm
He's been my strong salvation
In great calamity
He brought me out into green pastures
For He delighted in me

6. I've set the LORD before me
    Kept all His commands
    And He has well rewarded
    My pure heart and clean hands
    I have kept the ways of God
    I have not strayed from His side
    The wicked keep moving and shifting
    But with Him I will abide

7. To the kind He is kind
    To the pure He is pure
    To the upright He's blameless
    And all His mercies are sure
    But to the crooked and proud
    They only know His dread
    He saves a humble people
    But He kills them wicked dead

8. You light up my lamp
    You chase away my night
    Though a host should come against me
    I'll be filled with Your might
    My God, His way, it is perfect
    And every word of His is true
    My LORD, You're a shield and a refuge
    For every man who trusts in You

9. Who is God, but the LORD?
    Is there a rock like You?
    If You train my hands for war
    What can my enemies do?
    You set my feet securely
    I'm like a deer upon the heights
    I bend back my bow of solid bronze
    And set the wicked in my sights

10. Your salvation's my shield
    And my support is Your hand
    My feet won't slip or stumble
    In such a broad and stable land
    Your gentleness and mercy
    It's what has made me great
    Your way is sure before me
    And all my paths are good and straight

11. I'll run down my foes
    They will all be consumed
    When they see me coming
    They'll know that they are doomed
    And though they cry out for help
    Still they'll fall beneath my feet
    To the wind I'll scatter their ashes
    And drag their bodies through the streets

12. You've delivered me from strife
    Put the nations in my sway
    And though they have not known me
    I know that they'll obey
    They come to me and they tremble
    Down on their hands and on their knees
    I receive them into my service
    I'm accepting of their pleas

13. The LORD is my refuge
    And blessed be my Rock
    A good and faithful Shepherd
    Who saves His little flock
    He delivers us from evil
    And takes away our enemies
    He rescues us from the violent
    And puts our restless hearts at ease

14. I'll praise You to the heathen
    Declare to them Your fame
    You bring Your king salvation
    And Jesus is His name
    And now I'll praise His name forever
    And bring to Him my offerings
    Jesus loves and cares for His children
    He's our gracious King of kings

Satisfy My Soul
— PSALM 19 —

♩ = 126

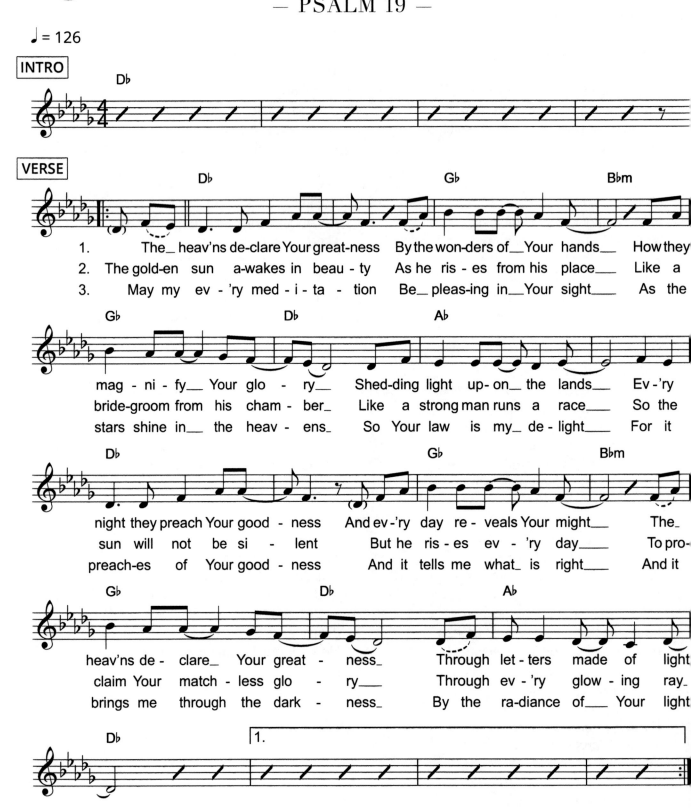

INTRO

Db

VERSE

Db   Gb   Bbm

1. The_ heav'ns de-clare Your great-ness   By the won-ders of__ Your hands__   How they
2. The gold-en sun a-wakes in beau - ty   As he ris - es from his place__   Like a
3. May my ev -'ry med - i - ta - tion   Be_ pleas-ing in__ Your sight__   As the

Gb   Db   Ab

mag - ni - fy__ Your glo - ry__   Shed-ding light up-on_ the lands__   Ev -'ry
bride-groom from his cham - ber_   Like a strong man runs a race__   So the
stars shine in__ the heav - ens_   So Your law is my_ de - light__   For it

Db   Gb   Bbm

night they preach Your good - ness   And ev -'ry day re - veals Your might__   The_
sun will not be si - lent   But he ris - es ev -'ry day__   To pro-
preach-es of Your good - ness   And it tells me what_ is right__   And it

Gb   Db   Ab

heav'ns de - clare_ Your great - ness_   Through let - ters made of light
claim Your match - less glo - ry__   Through ev -'ry glow - ing ray_
brings me through the dark - ness_   By the ra-diance of__ Your light

Db   1.

Lyrics by NATHAN ALBERSON and PHILIP MOYER. Music by PHILIP MOYER.

Satisfy My Soul
— PSALM 19 —

1. The heav'ns declare Your greatness By the wonders of Your hands How they magnify Your glory Shedding light upon the lands Ev'ry night they preach Your goodness And ev'ry day reveals Your might The heav'ns declare Your greatness Through letters made of light

2. The golden sun awakes in beauty As he rises from his place Like a bridegroom from his chamber Like a strong man runs a race So the sun will not be silent But he rises ev'ry day To proclaim Your matchless glory Through ev'ry glowing ray

3. May my ev'ry meditation Be pleasing in Your sight As the stars shine in the heavens So Your law is my delight For it preaches of Your goodness And it tells me what is right And it brings me through the darkness By the radiance of Your light

Lyrics by NATHAN ALBERSON and PHILIP MOYER. Music by PHILIP MOYER.

Some Trust in Horses
— PSALM 20 —

Verse lyrics:

1. May the LORD an-swer you in the day of wor-ry May the name of Ja-cob's God
2. When you bring of-fer-ings, may He find them pleas-ant Share with you all good things
3. We will hope for vic-to-ry and not be dis-ap-point-ed In the name of Ja-cob's God,

bless you from on high May He bring help to you from His sanc-tu-ar-y
when you come in-quire May He give help to you from the high-est heav-en
raise our ban-ners high For we know the LORD will come res-cue His a-noint-ed

May the LORD give to you the strength of Zion
May the LORD do for you what you de-sire
Bow the heav-ens down and make our foes to fly

CHORUS

Some will trust in char-i-ots Some will trust in hors-es We will boast in the name
of the LORD, our God We will rise, we will stand We will lift our voic-es
We will boast in the name of the LORD, our God

To Coda

46

Lyrics and music by JODY KILLINGSWORTH

Some Trust in Horses
— PSALM 20 —

CAPO V

♩ = 105

INTRO C

VERSE

Am / G / C / F / Am / G

1. May the LORD an-swer you in the day of wor-ry May the name of Ja-cob's God
2. When you bring of-fer-ings, may He find them pleas-ant Share with you_ all good things
3. We will hope for vic-to-ry and not be dis-ap-point-ed In the name of Ja-cob's God,

C / F F / G / C / F

bless you from on high May He bring help to you from His sanc-tu-ar-y
when you come in-quire May He give help to you from the high-est heav-en
raise our ban-ners high For we know the LORD will come res-cue His_ a-noint-ed

Am / G / F / C

May the LORD give to you_ the strength of Zion
May the LORD do for you_ what you de-sire
Bow the heav-ens down and make our foes to fly

CHORUS C / F / C / C

Some will trust in char-i-ots Some will trust in hors-es_ We will boast in the name

C / G / Am / F / C

of the LORD, our God We will rise, we will stand We will lift_ our voic-es_

C / G / C

To Coda

We will boast in the name of the LORD, our God

48 Lyrics and music by JODY KILLINGSWORTH

Hear Us When We Call
— PSALM 20 —

Lyrics by JAKE MENTZEL. Music by JODY KILLINGSWORTH.

CPSIA information can be obtained
at www.ICGtesting.com
Printed in the USA
LVOW09s2243230217

525292LV00001B/1/P